Who ruinec

As the Clue Crew got closer, they saw a large crowd outside the entrance of the tent. . . .

All three girls gasped. From what Nancy could see, it looked like someone went wild with the paint. Several of the bottles had been opened up and poured out onto the ground, causing the grass to turn all kinds of crazy colors! One table was ruined and a few of the pumpkins had fallen to the ground too, with some splitting open. Little globs of pumpkin goo covered some of the tables and grass, where they had opened up.

"Oh my gosh!" Bess cried. "Who could have done this?"

Join the CLUE CREW & solve these other cases!

#1 *Sleepover Sleuths*

#2 *Scream for Ice Cream*

#3 *Pony Problems*

#4 *The Cinderella Ballet Mystery*

#5 *Case of the Sneaky Snowman*

#6 *The Fashion Disaster*

#7 *The Circus Scare*

#8 *Lights, Camera . . . Cats!*

#9 *The Halloween Hoax*

#10 *Ticket Trouble*

#11 *Ski School Sneak*

#12 *Valentine's Day Secret*

#13 *Chick-napped!*

#14 *The Zoo Crew*

#15 *Mall Madness*

#16 *Thanksgiving Thief*

#17 *Wedding Day Disaster*

#18 *Earth Day Escapade*

#19 *April Fool's Day*

#20 *Treasure Trouble*

#21 *Double Take*

#22 *Unicorn Uproar*

#23 *Babysitting Bandit*

#24 *Princess Mix-up Mystery*

#25 *Buggy Breakout*

#26 *Camp Creepy*

#27 *Cat Burglar Caper*

#28 *Time Thief*

#29 *Designed for Disaster*

#30 *Dance off*

#31 *Make-a-Pet Mystery*

#32 *Cape Mermaid Mystery*

Nancy Drew and the Clue Crew®

#33

The Pumpkin Patch Puzzle

By Carolyn Keene

Illustrated by Macky Pamintuan

Aladdin
New York London Toronto Sydney New Delhi

If you purchased this book without a cover, you should be aware that this book is stolen property. It was reported as "unsold and destroyed" to the publisher, and neither the author nor the publisher has received any payment for this "stripped book."

This book is a work of fiction. Any references to historical events, real people, or real locales are used fictitiously. Other names, characters, places, and incidents are the product of the author's imagination, and any resemblance to actual events or locales or persons, living or dead, is entirely coincidental.

ALADDIN
An imprint of Simon & Schuster Children's Publishing Division
1230 Avenue of the Americas, New York, NY 10020
First Aladdin paperback edition September 2012

Designed by Lisa Vega
The text of this book was set in ITC Stone Informal.
Manufactured in the United States of America 1115 OFF
10 9 8 7 6 5 4
Library of Congress Control Number 2012932253
ISBN 978-1-4169-9465-7
ISBN 978-1-4424-5715-7 (eBook)

CONTENTS

The Pumpkin Patch Puzzle

CHAPTER ONE

Festival Fun

"Ugh, I can't wait for the end of the day!" exclaimed eight-year-old Nancy Drew.

"We have important things to do," added her friend Bess Marvin.

"Well, let's try to have fun and maybe the school day will go by faster!" said George Fayne.

It was a couple of days before the kickoff to the annual Fall Festival in River Heights. The festival was the highlight of the year for most, if not all, of the River Heights residents. There were all kinds of rides, games, food, and different fall-themed events for a week. The biggest part of the festival was the pumpkin decorating contest, which was on the first day of the festival. On the last day, the winner was announced—and would have the honor of having his or her design on all the banners and ads for next year, when the festival would be celebrating its fiftieth anniversary! The contest was open to kids as young as eight years old, and this was the first year that Nancy, Bess, and George would be entering.

"I can't wait to decorate our pumpkins," said George. "I need to start thinking of my design."

The girls were going to Nancy's house right after school to begin planning how to decorate their pumpkins. In order to be in the contest, anyone who wanted to compete had to submit their design idea to the festival committee by that Friday, before the festival's opening day and the actual contest, which would be on Saturday. The girls couldn't wait!

"Maybe I'll make mine look like a lion or tiger," George continued. "I think that would look really cool on a pumpkin."

"You want to put a big cat on your pumpkin? How dumb is that?"

The girls turned and saw Deirdre Shannon, one of their classmates—and one of the meaner girls at school—sitting at the cluster of desks right behind them.

"It's not dumb, Deirdre. Besides, you probably don't even *have* an idea for your design," said Bess.

"Whatever, girls," Deirdre said. "But you all better watch out, because I'm winning that contest *and* you will have to look at my design for the whole festival next year!"

"Just ignore her, Bess," Nancy said reassuringly as Deirdre turned around to chat with the rest of the kids in her group. "I think your idea could be really cool, George!"

Bess sighed. "I still don't know what to do. I really want my design to be the winning one—I mean, I want you guys to maybe win too," she added quickly.

Nancy and George laughed. "Well, hopefully everything will stay quiet around here so we can concentrate on our designs," Nancy said.

Nancy, Bess, and George were known around town for helping to solve mysteries in River Heights. Not only were they best friends (and George and Bess were cousins), they also had their own detective agency. They called themselves the Clue Crew—and had a pretty good success rate! Even though the girls were very different—Nancy was levelheaded, George was considered the "computer geek," and Bess was very fashion-conscious—they worked perfectly together and made a great team!

The girls chatted as they settled into their desks. But instead of the normal start with reading assignments, their principal, Mr. Newman, came in with a girl Nancy, George, and Bess had never seen before.

"Oh, I wonder if we have a new girl in class," whispered Nancy.

"Good morning, everyone!" said Mrs. Ramirez. "I want you all to give a big River Heights Elementary welcome to Emma

Costello. She just moved here from California and will be in class with you all."

Emma had big green eyes and curly brown hair. She was wearing a fun pink-and-brown dress, and cute shoes. She seemed a little nervous as she looked out at her new classmates.

"That must be hard moving all the way from California," said Bess.

"Hey, maybe she can come over after school and decorate some pumpkins with us," said Nancy. "That way, she can meet some more kids from class—and see the best part about the festival!"

Finally, the end-of-day bell rang, and the three girls hurried off toward their lockers to grab their things before heading over to Nancy's house. They were ready to start sketching out their ideas, and thought doing a little practice run on their own pumpkins would be a good idea before the big day. Besides Bess and George, Nancy had invited a few other classmates to come over as well.

"Hey, guys! Are you on your way to Nancy's house?" Violet Keeler called out.

"Yup! We're just waiting for Hannah to come pick us up so we can walk back with her," explained Bess. Hannah Gruen was the longtime housekeeper and family friend to the

Drews', and a second mom to Nancy. "I'm not sure if we are waiting for anyone else."

At that moment, Nancy came to the lockers where the girls were standing.

"We have one more—everyone, you remember Emma," Nancy said. "I thought it would be cool if she could decorate the pumpkins with us!"

"Hi, Emma! Do you know what you want to do with your pumpkin?" asked Bess.

Emma shrugged. "Um, I'm not really sure," she said. "I'm not a big fall person." She pushed a stray brown curl out of her face.

"Aw, well, I'm sure you'll think of something once we get started," said George.

Emma frowned. "Whatever—it's cool of Nancy to invite me over, but I'm not really into this whole festival thing. I think it's stupid!"

"Oh, look, there's Hannah," Nancy said, sounding relieved at the interruption. "Let's get this show on the road."

As the rest of the group chatted during the walk, with Hannah keeping a close eye on everything, Bess and George pulled Nancy aside.

"Nancy, it's nice of you to invite her, but I don't think she's going to have a very good time," said Bess. "Emma is kind of . . . rude."

"Well, she's just getting used to River Heights," Nancy pointed out. "It's not easy being the new girl. So maybe she'll be better once she gets to know everyone."

Suddenly a few of the girls screamed. "Look out! There's a ghost coming right at us!"

CHAPTER TWO

Decorating Drama

Nancy, Bess, and George ran toward the front of the group, with Hannah close behind. Sure enough, a small figure, all in white and with a scary face, was standing a few feet away. But as Nancy got closer, she realized it wasn't a ghost at all.

"Audrey! What are you doing?" yelled Emma.

The ghost girl took off her face—well, her mask. "You promised you would hang out with me after you got home from school. But it looks like you are just too busy for me," Audrey said with a huff.

Emma sighed. "Everyone, this is my little sister, Audrey. Audrey, these are some of the

kids from class. What are you doing out here?"

Audrey pointed. "Aunt Claire is at the store across the street. I saw you coming down the road and figured I'd scare you with my Halloween costume."

Hannah laughed. "I guess it worked pretty well!" No one else seemed to find it as funny as she did.

"Audrey? What are you doing?" A woman, dressed in jeans and a sweater, ran toward the group.

"I was trying to scare Emma and her friends, but it didn't work so well," said Audrey.

Aunt Claire groaned. "Audrey, I need you to behave. You know I have a lot going on, especially with festival planning." She glanced at Hannah and the group. "Sorry, everyone. I hope Audrey didn't startle you too much!"

"Wait, you're Emma's aunt?" asked Nancy, throwing a surprised glance at Emma. "You run the festival; that's so cool! I'm Nancy," she added. "We're about to go to my house and practice our designs for the pumpkin decorating contest."

Aunt Claire smiled. "Nice to meet you, Nancy. And yes, I've been the head of the festival for a few years now—I'm excited that Emma and Audrey finally get to be here for one."

"Our parents work for a newspaper, and they had to go to London for an assignment. They'll be gone for a whole year," Emma said. "So we got stuck moving here."

Aunt Claire forced another smile. "It'll be fun having my nieces out here, but I know it will been hard for them. So it's nice to see that Emma is finally making some new friends in town."

Nancy, Bess, and George exchanged glances. Somehow, they didn't think Emma felt the same way.

"Well, I guess I'll let you girls get cracking on your designing. Emma, you'll be home by five thirty, okay?"

Emma just rolled her eyes. "Yup, I'll be home. Don't worry, Aunt Claire, I know you're busy."

Aunt Claire took Audrey's hand. "Great! See you later! And nice meeting you all," she added as she and Audrey walked in the opposite direction.

Emma stared after her aunt and sister.

"I didn't know that your aunt was in charge of the entire festival—that's so awesome!" said Nancy.

Emma whirled around. "You wouldn't think it's so awesome if your aunt never had time to hang out because she has all this stupid festival stuff to do. It's awful!"

Nancy blinked in surprise at Emma's outburst, not really knowing what to say.

"Well, why don't we keep moving along before it gets too late," Hannah said hastily. "I'm sure your parents will all want you home before dinner!"

When the girls arrived at the Drew household, the mood lightened immediately. A row of pumpkins stood waiting in the sunroom, along with all sorts of special markers, glue, and stickers that the girls could use to decorate them.

"Wow, this is great! Thank you, Hannah, for setting this all up," Bess exclaimed.

"Of course! If any of you need anything, I'll be right in the next room," said Hannah.

Everyone started rummaging through the various supplies. Pretty soon glitter, paper, and markers were flying everywhere.

"I think I'm going to make mine look like a MusicMate, that cool new music player," said George. "Everyone is going to have something that looks like a face—I think mine will really stand out!"

"Ohhhh, good idea, George!" exclaimed Sonia, another of the girls' classmates. "It's right up your alley."

"I'm not sure what I want to do yet," said Madison Foley. "But I really, really want my design to win!"

George looked at her curiously. "Well, that's what we are all hoping for," she pointed out.

Madison sighed. "Well, there's this special arts camp that I want to go to this summer," she explained. "They don't have that many spots, so I'm hoping that I win the contest so I can get in!"

Bess grinned. "Aw, Madison, you're really good at drawing and stuff. I'm sure you can get in just on your own, without the festival competition."

Madison shook her head. "I'm not sure. I just want to really stand out, you know?"

The girls continued to chat as they started to make headway on their designs. Bess was hard at work on a princess-looking pumpkin, with a gold felt crown near the top of the pumpkin

and pretty glitter accents all over. George was doing well constructing the MusicMate pumpkin, complete with headphones for ears. And Nancy was busy making her pumpkin look like her beloved dog, Chocolate Chip! Even though George thought anything with a face was too common, Nancy thought her dog was just too cute to pass up. With a real button for the nose, colorful "fur" marks, and a sparkling, glittery tongue, who could resist the cuteness that was Chip?!

Nancy glanced over at the

rest of the girls. Everyone seemed to be having lots of fun—especially since Hannah had just brought in a plate of her superdelicious, super-special double-chocolate-chip cookies for a snack!

"You need to keep your energy up with all this decorating," Hannah had said.

But the only person who still looked glum was Emma, who seemed annoyed about something.

Nancy made her way over to the new girl.

"How do you like River Heights so far?" Nancy asked as she drew sparkly whiskers on her Chip pumpkin.

Emma sighed as she drew random curlicues all over her pumpkin. "You girls seem nice, but this is all dumb to me. My aunt only cares about this stupid festival. I wish I was back in California!"

Across the table, a few of the girls scowled.

"Geez, Emma, if you don't like it so much, you should just go back," Sonia said with a sniff.

"Yeah, we've tried to be nice, but you don't seem to care. I bet you'll win just because your aunt is in charge!" added Abby Warner, another classmate.

Emma glared at Abby. "It doesn't matter; I can't 'officially' enter since my aunt is involved with the festival. But if I could, I would definitely beat you guys!"

By the looks on the girls' faces, nobody thought so.

Just then Hannah bustled in.

"Okay, girls, time to wrap things up! Your parents are on their way."

"Just in time—things weren't looking too good," George whispered to Nancy.

As everyone said good-bye, Nancy wondered if Emma would ever find a friend in River Heights.

CHAPTER THREE

Pumpkin Possibilities

The next day, Nancy woke up to a delicious smell coming from the kitchen. "Nancy! Wake up! I've made a special breakfast for you," Carson Drew called up to his daughter.

"Coming, Daddy!" yelled Nancy as she bounded down the stairs.

A fresh stack of pancakes sat in the middle of the kitchen table, along with some butter and syrup. There were two plates, with a glass of juice at one place setting and a cup of coffee for Mr. Drew at the other.

Nancy grinned as she took a seat. "Yum! Pancakes! What's this for?" she asked as she took a few from the stack.

Mr. Drew smiled as he flipped the next batch of pancakes at the stove. "Well, Hannah had the morning off, and I know today is the day you bring your designs down to the folks at the festival. And it's Friday! Always a good day for pancakes."

Nancy giggled. "*Every* day is a good day for pancakes!" she said.

After the last batch was done, Nancy told her father a little about Emma and Audrey, and how their aunt was in charge of the festival. She also mentioned what had happened the day before.

"I just don't know what else to do, Daddy," Nancy said. "I've tried to be nice to her, but she isn't really making it easy to like her."

Carson smiled. "Give her a little more time, Nancy," he said. "It's hard moving, and she probably misses her mom and dad. Just keep being nice to her, so she knows she at least has one friend here."

Nancy sighed. "Okay. I'll keep trying," she said.

Carson grinned. "That's my girl! Now let's get you to school before you're late."

After the final bell rang, Nancy, Bess, and George all met in front of the school. Mrs. Fayne was on her way to drop the girls off at the main festival headquarters in downtown River Heights so they could submit their official design entry forms.

The girls could barely contain their excitement as they waited for George's mom. They protectively clutched their entry forms, which were sealed in envelopes with their names and ages on the front. They saw a few of their other classmates with their entries as well.

Soon, Mrs. Fayne's car pulled into view.

"You girls ready to go?" she asked with a smile. "I bet one of you will have the winning design!"

"I hope so, Mom!" exclaimed George.

As they got closer to downtown, a lot of the roads were already blocked off in preparation for the event. The banner proclaiming that it was the forty-ninth annual River Heights Fall Festival was being hung across the front of town hall. The girls all squealed in excitement as soon as they saw it.

"Aghhh, it's not even all set up yet and I'm so excited!" Bess cried.

Mrs. Fayne chuckled. "Easy, girls! I need to find a place to park." She frowned. "I'm not sure if I'm going to be able to find a spot. I'll just drop you off at town hall, and then I'll circle around and pick you back up. Sound good?"

Nancy, Bess, and George all nodded as they pulled in front of the town hall doors.

"Now, just wait for me there—don't go wandering anywhere," Mrs. Fayne said.

The girls went to the front check-in desk, where the kind town clerk pointed them toward the room where they needed to submit their forms.

"Good luck!" she called after them.

As the girls went into the room, Emma's aunt

Claire was busy taking entries from some of the kids who had already come through.

"Excuse me, Miss Costello? We're here to drop off our designs," Nancy said.

Aunt Claire glanced up. She smiled when she saw the Clue Crew.

"Hi there, girls!" she said. "How are you doing? Do you have your forms?"

Nancy, George, and Bess all nodded as they handed over their designs.

Remembering what her father had said earlier, Nancy said, "It was a lot of fun hanging out with Emma yesterday after school. It must be hard to move so far from home."

Aunt Claire smiled. "Yes, it's been difficult for her and Audrey. But I'm sure she'll settle in once she's been here a little bit longer. It's never easy being the new girl. And I know it's been hard to be away from their mom and dad."

Nancy nodded. "Well, I hope she and I can hang out again soon! See you tomorrow at the festival!"

"Thanks, Nancy. Actually, Emma is in the back somewhere, helping out with getting all the supplies ready, if you want to say hi." She turned away briefly to help someone who had just come in.

"Okay, girls, I need to get back to work. Good luck!" Aunt Claire went back to handling the forms as George, Bess, and Nancy started to leave.

"Let's see if we can find Emma," Nancy said. "Maybe she'll be in a better mood today." Besides, with all the excitement in the air, how could anyone not be happy about the festival?

Just as Nancy, Bess, and George went to go look, Emma hurried out of one of the back rooms with a box of various colored paints in little tubes. Her little sister, Audrey, trailed behind with small bags of paintbrushes.

"Hey, Emma!" Bess called out. "Do you need any help with that?"

Startled, Emma stopped midstride. "Oh hi,

guys. Um, sure, I guess that would be nice. I need to take these out back to the staging area, under the tents."

Nancy, Bess, and George each took a few bottles out of the box to lighten the load.

"Are you excited about tomorrow?" Nancy asked. "It looks so cool already."

Emma shrugged. "Kind of. I've actually been helping out Aunt Claire a lot with it, so maybe I'll be more into it once I don't have to carry boxes everywhere."

George laughed.

"Yeah, I can see why it would be a little different for you," she said. "It is a lot of work to put on the festival!"

Audrey frowned. "Yeah, she's made us do a lot of stuff for it." Her face brightened a little. "But since she hasn't had time to cook, we get to have pizza almost every night for dinner. So that's at least a good thing."

Everyone laughed at that—even Emma, who cracked the first real smile that Nancy had seen on her since she met her.

The girls finally got to the area where the pumpkin decorating contest would be held the next morning. Emma unzipped the entrance to a large, white tent. Inside, long tables were set side by side, with two big tables in the middle filled with what looked like a billion pumpkins.

"Wow, look at all those pumpkins!" exclaimed Bess. "I've never seen so many, except when I went on a hayride once."

Nancy and George smiled. They were definitely psyched for the festival to start!

"Hopefully it won't rain tomorrow," Emma said. "But at least we won't get wet if it does."

They set down the supplies on the tables that ran around the outer edges of the tents. Stacks of chairs were scattered all around, waiting to get put out.

"Do you need help setting anything up?" Nancy asked.

Emma shook her head. "Nah, we have to get here superearly tomorrow morning to help set up all the paint bottles on each table. We have some bags of stickers and stuff too, in case people want to use those. But thanks for helping us carry all this out."

George grinned. "No problem, Emma. We'll see you tomorrow morning."

"Bye, everyone! Good luck tomorrow with your pumpkins," Audrey called out.

As the girls were heading out the door, Deirdre, Tommy Sassano, and Stacy Quinn were just coming in to drop off their entries.

"Oh, look, it's the Boring Crew," Deirdre said.

George frowned.

"What did you guys end up doing for each of your designs? That stupid tiger?" Deirdre continued, looking at George. "Only babies would do that."

"Actually, George has a really cool idea, Deirdre," Nancy said. "So I'd watch out if I were you!"

Deirdre and Stacy laughed, but not Tommy, who just stared at Nancy with an annoyed expression on his face. "Whatever, Clueless Crew." Dierdra sneered. "It's going to be one of us winning that design contest—it's a done deal!"

Before anyone could say anything, Mrs. Fayne pulled up to the entrance.

"Ready, girls?" she called out.

"Oh yeah!" replied Bess.

She turned back to Deirdre, who was still standing there.

"May the best design win tomorrow," Bess added. "Hopefully it won't be yours!"

CHAPTER FOUR

Dashed Dreams

It was finally opening day of the River Heights Fall Festival! Nancy was up bright and early, too excited to stay in bed. Besides, the opening ceremony was at ten that morning, with the pumpkin decorating contest kicking off shortly thereafter.

When she got downstairs, Hannah was already busy at the stove making breakfast.

"Here you go, dear," Hannah said, sliding a plate of french toast and strawberries toward Nancy. "You need to have something before you get over to the festival."

Mr. Drew came downstairs a few minutes later.

"Eat up, honey. We need to get you over to the contest in a little bit. Are you excited?"

Nancy nodded. "I think Bess, George, and I have really cool design ideas. Besides, I want to check out the rest of the festival before the actual contest starts. I really want an apple-cider doughnut. Or an apple fritter!"

Hannah and her father laughed. "Well, eat most of your breakfast and you can get whatever you want—it's a special day," said Mr. Drew.

After Nancy finished eating, she went upstairs to change into an outfit she had picked out just for the festival—black pants and a sparkly orange top. She was going to look like her own pumpkin!

Mr. Drew, Hannah, and Nancy made their way to downtown River Heights.

Nancy gasped as the center of town came into view. It looked like people had done a *lot* of work overnight. Besides the banner, colorful lights and lanterns were hanging by all the light posts that lined Main Street. Food booths were set up, with delicious smells coming from them.

"Wow, Daddy! Look at all of this! It looks so great!" exclaimed Nancy.

He nodded. "It looks better and better every year," said Mr. Drew. "And I've been coming to the festival since I was your age."

Nancy giggled. "Were there dinosaurs as part of the festival then?"

Mr. Drew pretended to look shocked. "That's it! No treats for you, miss," he said, ruffling his hand through Nancy's hair. "It wasn't *that* long ago. We at least had horses and buggies then," he joked.

As Nancy, Hannah, and Mr. Drew kept walking, they bumped into George, Bess, and their families.

"Hi, guys! Doesn't this look awesome?" said George.

Bess, who already had a warm apple-cider doughnut in her hand, nodded in agreement.

"Let's walk around a little bit—we have time before the kickoff ceremony," said Nancy.

As the adults chatted, Nancy, Bess, and George took in all the sights and smells of the festival. They saw several of their classmates who were wandering around as well. There were booths set up with all kinds of arts and crafts for sale, along with vendors selling fun balloons and toys out of their carts. Even Yuks Joke Shop had their own cart, peddling all the whoopee cushions and itching powder anyone could want!

Though Bess had already sampled a treat, the girls made a beeline for the food booth that was selling warm apple fritters, a delicious tradition that had been a festival favorite since the very first year.

"Wow, these are so good!" Nancy sighed happily as she took her first bite.

After they finished their fritters, they still had some time to kill. Nancy decided to go see how Emma was doing. Even though she hadn't been the nicest person, Nancy took her father's words to heart.

"I'll be right back," Nancy said. "Daddy, I'm going to say hi to Emma before everything starts."

Mr. Drew planted a quick kiss on the top of his daughter's head. "That's my girl," he said. "Tell her hi for me!"

Nancy weaved her way through some arts-and-crafts booths that were still setting up shop and finally made it into the pumpkin tent.

Emma and Audrey were setting up all the supplies, including the bottles that Nancy, Bess, and George had helped bring in the day before. The tent was even decorated, and it truly felt like it was time to start the pumpkin games!

Emma finally noticed Nancy standing there.

"Oh hey, Nancy! We were just finishing up with the setup. Would you mind helping?"

"Sure," Nancy said as she grabbed a few bottles of paint.

Suddenly the girls heard the crackling of a loud-speaker coming to life, and the voice of Mayor Strong boomed out over the festival grounds.

"Everyone! If you could all make your way to the main stage here, we are just about ready to kick off the forty-ninth annual River Heights Fall Festival!"

"Let's go see!" said Nancy.

Emma waved her on. "Don't worry, I actually have a lot more to set up here. But I'll see you later. Thanks for coming by to say hi!" She smiled and went back to putting out more supplies.

People began making their way over to the town green, where a large stage had been set up. Nancy spotted Bess and George and ran over to join them. Mayor Strong was there, along with the Festival Fairies and their queen. The fairies and queen were a group of local high school girls who were chosen to be the faces of the festival each year, and it was a big deal. They even got to ride in supercool cars in the festival parade!

Nancy, Bess, and George tried to get as close as possible to the front of the stage. But the small space quickly filled up with a bunch of people doing the exact same thing!

As they tried to make their way to the front, Nancy bumped into their classmates Lea Rell and Shelby Metcalf.

"Hi, girls! Are you excited for the contest?"

Lea nodded. "Yeah! I wish I could see everything, though," she complained. "There's too many people here."

Shelby stood on her tiptoes. "I think they'll be starting soon. I just want to get started on my pumpkin."

Nancy smiled. "What are you thinking of for a design?" she asked.

Shelby grinned. "You'll have to wait and see! But I really want to win this contest. I'd love for my design to be on all the posters next year!"

"Ha, I think we all do," Nancy replied with a laugh.

Just as Shelby was about to respond, the speakers crackled to life as Mayor Strong's voice boomed out again.

"Everyone, I'd like to welcome you all to the official opening of the River Heights Fall Festival! I'd like to thank the wonderful festival committee, led by Claire Costello, for putting on such a wonderful event for yet another year."

Everyone clapped as Aunt Claire waved to the crowd.

Mayor Strong continued with his remarks.

"And we can't forget her right-hand man, Rick Rickston, who organized all the super volunteers that you will see during the next week."

A tall man wearing khakis and a button-down shirt stepped forward and waved to the crowd.

After the applause died down, Mayor Strong took to the microphone once again.

"I know everyone is very excited to get started

with the main event—the pumpkin decorating contest! From what I have seen, we have some very creative young people here in River Heights."

The Clue Crew grinned. "I wish he would hurry it up already," George said anxiously. "I want to start on my pumpkin!"

"And now, after Miss Costello explains the rules, I'd like all the entered participants to head over to the pumpkin decorating area, right here behind town hall," Mayor Strong said with a smile. "Remember, the winning pumpkin design will be featured on all the ads and banners for next year's fiftieth-anniversary celebration of the Fall Festival! Good luck to everyone!"

As soon as Mayor Strong finished, Aunt Claire got up to say a few words.

"Before we start, I just want to give a few quick instructions about how the contest will work. Everyone gets just one pumpkin but can use whatever is on the table—we have paints, glitter, glue, everything to make your pumpkin look spook-tacular!"

The crowd chuckled as Aunt Claire continued. "And I want to remind everyone that the only way you are eligible is if you submitted your design by four p.m. yesterday to the committee for our review. We have a list of all the names of the eligible participants, so as soon as you get over to the contest area, please see one of the Festival Fairies to make sure your name is on the list!"

With that, Nancy, Bess, and George made their way over to the large tent.

"I'm kind of nervous—I hope I don't mess up," Bess said. "You only get one shot, since you only get to have one pumpkin!"

"I'm sure you'll be fine, Bess," Nancy said, reassuring her friend. "Just take your time. We have a few hours to complete everything."

As the Clue Crew got closer, they saw a large crowd outside the entrance of the tent. In the middle of the group, they could see some of the Festival Fairies and volunteers gesturing wildly. Nancy, Bess, and George pushed their way inside.

All three girls gasped. From what Nancy

could see, it looked like someone went wild with the paint. Several of the bottles had been opened up and poured out onto the ground, causing the grass to turn all kinds of crazy colors! One table was ruined and a few of the pumpkins had fallen to the ground too, with some splitting open. Little globs of pumpkin goo covered some of the tables and grass, where they had opened up.

"Oh my gosh!" Bess cried. "Who could have done this?"

CHAPTER FIVE

Pumpkin Problems

As the festival attendees all looked on, confused, Aunt Claire came bursting into the tent. She whistled to get everyone's attention.

"Okay, everyone. Can I have your attention for a minute? Did anyone see anything before they came in?" she demanded.

Everyone looked at one another. Most of the people had been enjoying the opening ceremonies and had been chatting with each other as they made their way to the pumpkin tent.

"I can't believe someone would do this on purpose," Bess whispered. "Who would want to ruin the festival?"

Nancy was thinking the same thing.

Aunt Claire continued. "I've also found out that all the design entries are missing. Someone has taken the entire box where I kept the forms!"

Groans came from the crowd. This was getting worse and worse.

Nancy noticed that more and more people were starting to make their way into the tent—including Mayor Strong. His eyes widened in shock as he saw the mess. He hurried over to Aunt Claire, his shoes making a weird slurping sound as he stepped in crushed pumpkin goo.

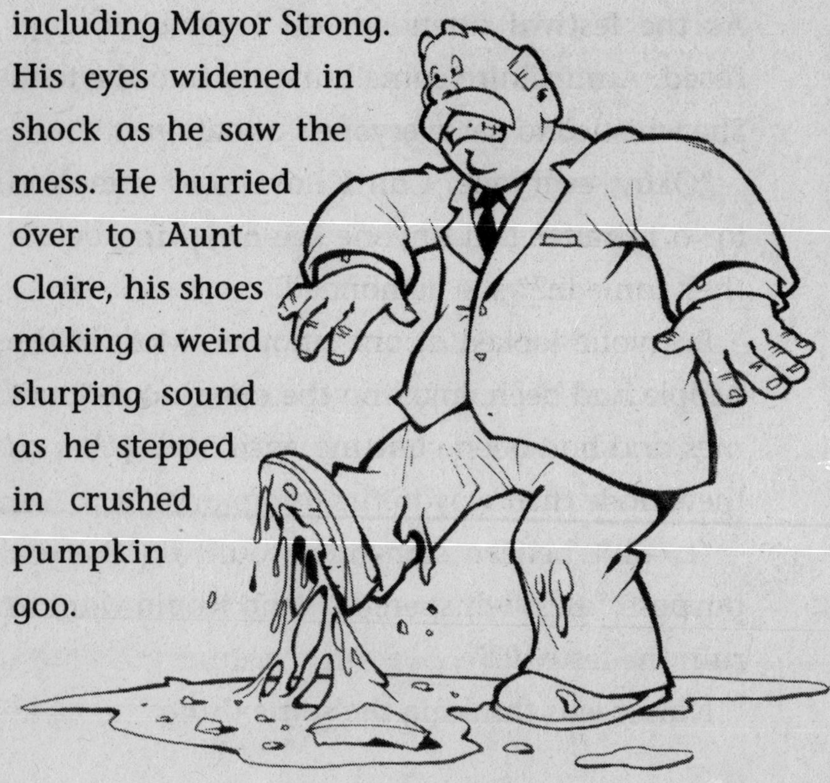

As she watched the commotion, Nancy sniffed the air. She could smell the faint scent of something sweet. Almost like a perfume, but stronger. It smelled familiar.

"Do you guys smell that?" Nancy asked.

George and Bess sniffed the air. "It smells like cookies," Bess said.

"It's probably just all the fair food that's around," George added.

Mayor Strong had finally gotten through the crowd and was talking loudly with Aunt Claire.

"Claire! What is going on here?" he asked, alarmed. "*When* did this even happen?"

Aunt Claire shrugged. "I was just asking people if they had seen anything," she explained. "This has never happened before. It looks like a disaster zone in here!"

Mayor Strong faced the crowd, who had started to chatter among themselves. "Everyone quiet!" he yelled. "Now, clearly, we will not be able to hold the pumpkin decorating contest today," he said as he gestured to the chaos around him. "If anyone can remember seeing or hearing anything, please come speak to either Miss Costello or Mr. Rickston.

"I've also been told by Miss Costello that all the entries seem to be missing as well." He paused as he gathered his last few thoughts. "Because of the serious nature of the vandalism here, I want to say this. If we cannot find out who did this by the end of the festival next week, the pumpkin decorating contest will have to be canceled."

Gasps and cries of "oh no!" echoed throughout the crowd.

Nancy turned to Bess and George. "This is awful," Nancy said. "I can't believe all our hard work might be for nothing!"

"And I really liked my design," Bess said sadly.

"We have to find out who is behind all of this," George said determinedly. "I think the Clue Crew is about to have another case!"

Nancy and Bess smiled. "Sounds good to me," Nancy said. "Let's help clean up here and see if we can find anything out before we start our official investigation."

The girls walked up to Aunt Claire, Emma, and Audrey.

"Oh hi, girls." Aunt Claire looked like she was about to cry. "I'm so sorry for all this. We're just going to clean up in here and try to figure out what happened."

"Well, we wanted to offer to help," Nancy said. "We've been able to solve a lot of cases around River Heights."

"It's true! The Clue Crew is really good at solving mysteries," Gina Gleason, one half of the Gleason twins, called as she walked out of the tent.

Aunt Claire managed a smile. "Well, thank you, girls, but I'm afraid this is probably a matter for the police. Whoever did this caused damage to what is technically town property, not to mention the fact that they ruined the most important part of the festival." She closed her eyes and took a deep breath.

Emma looked at her aunt with a worried expression. "Aunt Claire, are you okay?"

Aunt Claire opened her eyes and forced a smile. "I'll be okay, sweetie. Could you help me clean up this mess? I need to go talk to Mayor Strong and a few of the committee members for a bit."

She glanced at the Clue Crew. "Would you mind helping us clean up too? We need all the hands we can get. I'll grab some fritters and treats to thank you all."

Nancy grinned. "We were going to help anyway, but we'll always take fritters!"

Aunt Claire smiled. "I'll be back. Let one of the Festival Fairies know if you need anything, and they can come find me."

Nancy, Bess, George, and Emma started to throw pieces of crushed pumpkin into the big trash cans that had been set up around the tent. A few of their other classmates and fellow festival volunteers were trying to clean up the paint.

"Is it true that you guys really are detectives?" Emma asked.

Nancy nodded. "But I don't think your aunt wants our help," she said. Out of the corner of her eye, she saw Audrey listening in as she picked up an empty bottle nearby.

Emma sighed. "I feel bad that this happened. I know Aunt Claire has worked really hard on the festival."

Just as Nancy was about to respond, she frowned as she spotted a small, shiny object. It was partially covered in red paint that had spilled during the chaos.

She carefully lifted it up, wiping it off a bit in the grass. It was a small bracelet with a little gold star charm hanging off it.

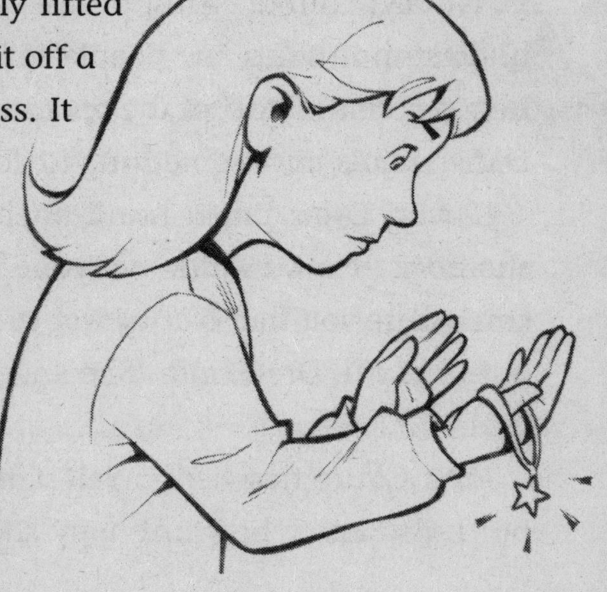

I wonder if this belongs

to the person who did this, Nancy thought. She slipped it into her sweater pocket for safe-keeping.

Just then Carson Drew and Hannah came into the tent.

"You okay, Nancy?" Mr. Drew asked. "This is an awful way to kick off the festival!"

"Well, hopefully they can find who did this, and soon," said Hannah.

Suddenly, Aunt Claire, Rick Rickston, and Mayor Strong burst back into the tent.

"Nancy! Emma!" Aunt Claire walked over. "I understand that a few people saw you both in here before the start of the opening ceremonies. Did you girls have something to do with this?"

Carson Drew put a hand on his daughter's shoulder. "Now, I know everyone is upset, but I can assure you that Nancy would never do such a thing," Mr. Drew said. "She knows better than that."

Aunt Claire frowned. "Well, Emma does too, but I also know how unhappy she's been," she said. "Emma? If you have something to say to me, you better say it now."

Emma stared at her aunt with an angry expression. "I can't believe that you think I would wreck your stupid festival!" she yelled. "All I've done is try to help you out all week, and then you think I would ruin it? I could have been listening to Bryce Brown's new album, but instead I was stuck here."

Aunt Claire's face softened. "I'm sorry, girls," she said. "But we have to explore every possibility here." She turned toward Mr. Drew and Nancy. "I hope you understand."

Carson and Nancy both nodded. "Why don't we walk around a little before we go home?" he suggested. "Let's try to enjoy a bit more of the festival, even though it got off to a rough start."

"Sure, one second, Dad."

As Aunt Claire and Mr. Drew walked out, Nancy stayed behind to talk to Emma.

"Emma, listen. I know you were helping out a lot with the festival and pumpkin contest, but are you sure you don't know what happened?" Nancy asked.

"Ugh, no! You're as bad as my aunt right now," she huffed. "Why don't you get together with your little detective agency and try to figure it out!" With that, she stormed off.

Nancy sighed. It looked like the Clue Crew definitely had themselves another case to solve!

Chapter Six

Tent Trouble

"Okay, so let's figure out our list of suspects," Nancy said.

After Nancy managed to find Bess and George, the three girls went over to Nancy's house with a bag full of apple-cider doughnuts and warm apple cider—perfect fuel for solving mysteries!

The Clue Crew gathered around Nancy's computer, where they opened up a new file to start listing the five *W*'s: who, what, when, where, why—and how.

"Ack, George, you're in my way," Bess complained. "I can't see anything!"

"Then move over," George replied. "I'm staying right where I am!"

Nancy held back a smile as she listened to the two cousins bicker.

"Okay, focus! Now, we're still not sure of our who," Nancy said.

"I still say it's Emma," Bess declared. "That girl totally had it out for this festival. I don't even think she likes pumpkins! Who doesn't like pumpkins?"

"Clearly, our suspect doesn't," Nancy said. "I don't really think Emma did it. She got very angry and upset when Aunt Claire and I both asked her—and she didn't look like she was lying."

"I still say we need to keep her on our list," George said.

"Well, what about Deirdre?" Bess pointed out as Nancy typed. "She seemed pretty sure that she would win."

"But why would she try to ruin it?" asked Nancy.

Bess thought for a moment. "Maybe she thought that by wrecking all the supplies or stealing the forms she could sneak in a different entry," she said. "Her design was probably dumb anyway, and she thought she could do a last-second change!"

Even though Nancy thought that possibility was a long shot, she dutifully typed in Deirdre's name on the suspect list.

"Ohhhh, and Madison Foley," George added. "Didn't she want to go to an arts camp this summer?"

"Good call, George," Nancy said. "Maybe she thought her design wouldn't be good enough after all."

As Nancy finished typing up some more notes, Hannah came into the room.

"Bess, George, your moms are both here to pick you up," she said. "It was nice seeing you girls today! I hope you had a good time, even with the competition being canceled.

George shrugged. "At least we got good treats out of the deal!"

Laughing, Hannah led George and Bess downstairs.

Nancy suddenly realized she had forgotten to mention the bracelet she had found earlier. As she added that to her notes, she wondered if there was any way they would be able to find the suspect in time to save the festival.

"I just don't get it, Daddy," Nancy said later as they enjoyed a pizza dinner from Nancy's favorite pizza place, Pizza Paradise. She sipped her water as she gathered the courage to ask her next question. "You don't really think I had anything to do with it, right?"

Mr. Drew put his napkin down. "Of course not, Nancy. Besides, if you had, I know you wouldn't be able to lie to me." He chuckled as he took another bite of his pepperoni pizza. "Even when you were little, your right eye would always twitch if you told a white lie."

Nancy laughed. "Thanks, Daddy. I knew you believed me, but I wanted to make sure. I think Bess, George, and I are going to try and help Miss Costello. She seemed really upset."

"Well, it's a big event for the town, and it was awful what happened," Mr. Drew said. "And you know you can always ask me for help if you need it."

After dinner, Nancy and her dad watched a TV show about baby animals in the wild. But Nancy was having a hard time paying attention, even though she loved animals—especially her dog, Chip, who was snuggled up to her on the couch.

I wonder if we'll be able to solve this case before next weekend, Nancy thought worriedly. *Our time is running out!*

"Are you sure this is going to work?" Bess asked after Mrs. Fayne dropped them off at the entrance to the fair.

The next day, the girls were on their way back to see if there were any other clues they could find. It was another beautiful fall day—perfect for doing some more investigating.

As the girls walked the short distance to the

center of the festival, Nancy explained the bracelet she found.

"It had a star charm on it? That doesn't give us much of a clue," Bess said.

Nancy shrugged. "I know, but maybe some-one will mention that it's missing. Let's go back to the pumpkin tent to see if anyone comes back for it."

The girls made their way to the tent, after a quick pit stop at the Patsy's Pastries cart for extra energy. The tent had already been blocked off with yellow tape so that the volunteers could clean up everything. They could hear music coming from inside as they got closer.

As Nancy, Bess, and George started through the entrance to the tent, a teenage boy wear-ing a T-shirt with "San Francisco" on it blocked their entrance.

"Sorry, this isn't open to the public and you can't come in here," San Francisco said. "We're still trying to clean up."

Nancy smiled at him. "We just wanted to pop

in for a second to see if anyone left a bracelet I found." She held out the small bracelet, which still had traces of red paint on it.

The boy shook his head. "Sorry, bosses' orders. Why don't you come back later?"

Dejected, the girls started to walk away.

As Nancy turned back, she noticed that San Francisco had started chatting with a friend. He wasn't paying attention at all.

"Hey! C'mon, there's another little opening on the other side of this tent," Nancy whispered.

The girls crept along the other side of the tent. Bess eased back the flap, and they all slipped in.

The place looked much better than yesterday. The tables were clean, and all the destroyed supplies had been thrown out. The long tables were empty, with only a few traces of various colors of paint splattered on them. The music the girls had heard earlier was coming from a MusicMate, which someone had plugged into a set of speakers—probably to help pass the time as everyone cleaned up.

Surprisingly, there weren't too many people in the tent. A young couple finished throwing a few things away and headed out the front of the tent, not even noticing that the girls had come in.

"Nancy, what are we looking for here?" asked George. "Everything has been thrown away!"

Nancy motioned for the girls to follow her over to one of five big garbage cans that were scattered around the tent. It didn't look like anyone had bothered to empty any of them since the day before.

Bess wrinkled her nose. "Ew, Nancy. I'm not

going in the garbage for clues!" she declared.

"Yeah, that's gross," George added.

Nancy sighed. "Guys, come on. Let's just take a peek in each one. You never know if you can find something."

The girls started peering into the cans, looking for something that might be helpful.

"Are you guys finding anything yet?" Bess called out.

"Nope—lots of wrappers, paper towels, and empty fritter bags!" Nancy replied.

After a few more minutes, George called out, "Hey! I think I have something." She plucked a piece of paper out of the garbage with the tips of her fingers. It was the application for KraftyKidz, a summer arts school. Though it was partially ripped, they could see that some of the information had already been filled out.

"Looks like there is an *S* in there somewhere, and an *F*, George said, squinting at the page.

"Hey! Didn't Madison Foley say she wanted to win so she could get into some sort of special art thing?" Bess asked. "I bet this is the program."

Could Madison be the person we're looking for? Nancy wondered. She really wanted to go to that school—maybe she decided to steal the designs so she would have more time to see what her competition would be like.

Suddenly the girls heard loud voices right outside the tent.

"Quick, we need to hide somewhere!" Nancy hissed. "We aren't supposed to be in here!"

"Where are we supposed to go?" asked Bess as they all hurried to the part of the tent farthest away from the front entrance.

The girls dove behind one of the big garbage cans and crouched down just as a pair of sparkly sneakers appeared in the tent.

CHAPTER SEVEN

Wrecked and Ripped

The sneakers stopped for a moment, then started straight toward the Clue Crew's hiding spot! As Nancy peeked out from behind the can, she saw that it was Shelby Metcalf.

"Shelby!" Nancy stood up from their hiding spot.

With a startled scream, Shelby jumped back.

"Nancy! What are you guys doing here?" she asked.

George and Bess stepped out too, their eyes narrowed. "We want to ask you the same thing, Shelby," George said. "Why are you sneaking back into the tent?"

"Did you have something to do with the stolen designs and the mess that happened here?" Bess added.

Shelby shook her head no. Her hair swayed back and forth.

"No, guys! I swear! I, um, came to get something that—that someone lost," she stammered.

Nancy's eyes widened. "You mean this?" she asked as she held out the charm bracelet.

Shelby looked confused. "Oh no, that's not mine," she said, curious. "It's pretty, though."

The Clue Crew exchanged glances. Shelby seemed like she was telling the truth. But why was she there?

"Listen, I'm actually here to help out

Madison," Shelby said. "She's one of my best friends, you know."

Bess, George, and Nancy nodded as Shelby continued. "Well, I guess a person from the camp was going to be at the festival, and she was going to give them her application form in person. But when she heard that all the designs got stolen, Madison got so upset and tore up her application and threw it out while we were in this tent."

Shelby tapped her sparkly foot. "She is really talented, and I think she can get in even without this design competition. I was going to try to find the form and have her sign up anyway."

George held up the ripped form. "Ugh, I think she will want a new one," she said with a giggle. "It has dried pieces of cotton candy on it!"

The girls all laughed as they started to make their way out of the tent.

"Now, what in the world is going on here?"

Aunt Claire was standing in the main opening to the tent, arms crossed, with a stern look on her face. Rick Rickston, the cochair, was also there, not looking too pleased either.

"We were just . . . leaving," Nancy said meekly.

"Actually, we were looking for clues that might help us find out who tried to ruin the pumpkin competition," George said. "We really want to finish the competition next weekend!"

Aunt Claire sighed. "Girls, I already told you that we are handling this on our own," she said. "I appreciate your help, but you need to leave this to the adults."

Shelby smiled. "I was just here trying to help my friend out," she said. "But it would be really cool if the Clue Crew could help!"

Nancy took a step toward Aunt Claire. "I think I might have found a clue, too," she said, showing her the gold star bracelet.

Aunt Claire looked at the bracelet with a curious expression. "Where did you find that, Nancy?" she asked.

Nancy pointed to the ground. "I found this while I was helping Emma clean up the mess," she said. "It was lying near one of the tables."

"Well, I'm sure it's nothing," Aunt Claire said dismissively. "Someone probably just lost it while we were all in here yesterday."

"Well, we're still happy to help you out if you want," Bess said.

Aunt Claire gave them all a tight smile. "I think you have done more than enough already, girls. Why don't you go enjoy the rest of the festival?"

With that, she motioned for Mr. Rickston to follow her out.

"I guess that's our cue, guys," Bess said. "We still have a little bit of time before my mom comes to pick us up. Let's go on some of the rides! Shelby, wanna come with us on a few?"

Shelby shook her head. "Sorry, I gotta go meet up with the rest of my family. They're over by the arts and crafts, and I snuck away while they were looking at new dog collars for our puppy. Some collars glow in the dark!"

The Clue Crew waved good-bye to Shelby as

they started toward the back parking lot, where some of the rides and games were set up.

"I want to try that Stomp-A-Squirrel game," George said enthusiastically. "I really want to win a new stuffed animal. Furrrocious needs a new friend!" Furrrocious is her (stuffed) pet bear that she had made with the girls at the Make-a-Pet store a little while ago.

"Do you mean Whac-A-Mole, George?" Nancy asked with a laugh.

"Whatever, you know what I mean! As long as there are animals I can win!" George shot back.

As the girls walked toward the main arcade, a strong gust of wind blew scraps of paper that had fallen on the ground nearby. Nancy picked one up. As she studied it, a look of recognition came over her face.

"Nancy, what is it?" Bess asked. "Where did that paper come from?"

"I think this is part of one of the entry forms for the decorating contest," Nancy said slowly. "Look!" She could make out the outline of a pumpkin, with one headphone over the side of the pumpkin.

"That looks like my MusicMate design!" George exclaimed.

The girls looked at the scraps of paper that were littering the ground. They began to follow the trail, picking up pieces as they went. Some had parts of designs, others were ripped right where the names were written.

As they walked along the paper path, the

pieces were a bit larger. Finally, right near River Heights First Bank was a large cardboard box.

"Oh my gosh, you guys! It's the missing design forms!" Nancy said.

The girls hurried over to the box. Inside were dozens of forms, some of them ripped, but most intact. As the girls started looking through the box, Nancy noticed a gold, shiny headband nearby that was a little dirty, probably from sitting out for hours.

Nancy picked up the headband. On the inside was a label that said "Dazzle Designs." It was a new boutique that had opened up on Main Street just a few months ago and was one of the coolest new stores in town. The headband was small and looked made for a girl Nancy's age—definitely not for a grown-up! The initials "D.S." were in black marker on the inside of the band.

"I think we have another clue," Nancy said as she held out the pretty hair accessory. "Maybe the same person who lost their bracelet lost this headband, too."

"Well, they sure like shiny things," George said.

Nancy held on to the band. "I guess I'll just keep this for now," she said. "I don't think I want to wear it. It's been on the ground for who knows how long!"

"Should we tell someone that we found the entry forms over here?" George asked as the girls finally made their way to the games.

Nancy shook her head. "Miss Costello didn't look too happy when we tried to ask her about it in the tent," she said. "Maybe we can just keep searching and then show her what we have once we have more information."

As they walked toward the big Slammin' Slide, a huge slide that you race down with one other person, the girls spotted Deirdre Shannon and her little group of friends.

"Oh, look, it's the Crazy Crew," Deirdre said. Suddenly she stopped short as she stared at the headband in Nancy's hand.

"Hey! What are you doing with that?" Deirdre demanded. "That's my headband, Drew!"

Chapter Eight

Dazzling Dilemma

Nancy, Bess, and George all stared at Deirdre in shock.

"So you're the one who ruined the whole festival!" George shouted.

"I knew you would try to do something like this," Bess added.

Deirdre looked at them, confused. "Wait, what? I didn't have anything to do with that mess that happened yesterday. I lost my headband a few days ago and have been going crazy looking for it! It's my favorite new accessory," she added.

The Clue Crew exchanged glances. "But you said yourself that you knew you were going to win," Nancy said. "Why should we believe you?"

Deirdre rolled her eyes. "I said I knew I would win because I knew that my design would totally beat whatever dumb ideas you guys came up with," she said, as if it were obvious.

"But we found your hair band right near—" George let out an "oof" as Bess elbowed her in the side.

"Near what?" Deirdre asked suspiciously.

"Uh . . . near some top-secret stuff," Bess said.

Deirdre rolled her eyes again. "Whatever. Can I just have my headband back?" she asked, holding out her hand.

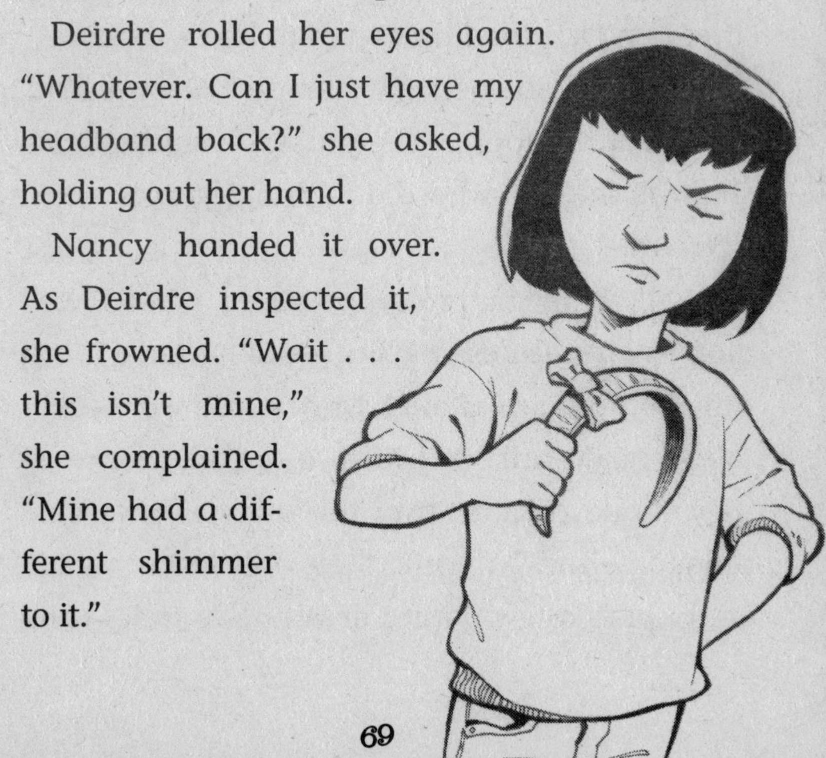

Nancy handed it over. As Deirdre inspected it, she frowned. "Wait . . . this isn't mine," she complained. "Mine had a different shimmer to it."

George elbowed Bess back, a little harder than necessary. "She can tell by the shimmer?" she asked in disbelief.

Deirdre looked it over some more. "Oh well. It's a pretty headband. I'd keep it anyway, but I don't know where it's been!"

With that, she threw the headband at Nancy and walked away without a backward glance, trailed closely by her friends.

"Gee, thanks, Deirdre!" Nancy called out after her. Deirdre didn't seem to hear—or care.

"Ohhhhh, she gets me so mad," George said, stomping her foot in the grass. "I kind of wish she was the one who did it. She deserves to get in trouble!"

"Well, I guess that's one more person who didn't steal the designs. But we don't have much time left to figure it out," Nancy said worriedly.

The girls walked a little more in silence as they made their way to the games. They had time to do the Slammin' Slide only once, but did get to play a few games of Whac-A-Mole—and

George won a little stuffed lion so Furrrocious could have a friend!

Finally it was time to go, and as the girls waited for Mrs. Marvin to pick them up, they discussed the new things they had discovered at the fair.

"Well, at least we know where the box of designs is," George said.

"But I feel like we still aren't close to figuring out who did it," Bess said, disappointed. "All we really have is that gold charm bracelet that Nancy found and the gold headband that we aren't sure who it belongs to."

As the girls rode home, they knew that one thing was for sure—time was running out and they needed to figure out who did this, and fast!

On Monday, all anyone could talk about at school was the ruined pumpkin contest on Saturday. Emma looked even more miserable than usual.

"My aunt has been in such a bad mood ever since Saturday," Emma told Nancy at lunch later that day. Nancy had asked her to come sit with her, George, and Bess to try and cheer her up—and maybe get some more information.

Emma pulled an apple from her bag and made a face. "Ugh. I don't even want to look at an apple right now!"

"Your aunt didn't seem too happy to see us," George said. They had told Emma about the tent mishap on Sunday and how her aunt still didn't want them to help out.

"Aunt Claire is just upset," Emma said. "She doesn't do anything but sit on her phone all day now and talk to people from the Fall Festival committee. She said it's making her look bad."

Nancy exchanged glances with George and Bess.

"Emma, there's something that we think you might want to know," Nancy said. "We actually found the stolen design forms on Sunday too."

Emma looked shocked as she dropped her unwanted (and uneaten) apple on the floor. As she bent down to pick it up, a sweet smell hit

Nancy's nose—the same scent that had been in the air on Saturday.

"Emma, what's that smell?" Nancy asked quickly. "It smells yummy!"

Confused, Emma looked at Nancy strangely. "Um, it's a new lotion from that bath shop at the mall—it's called Sugar Spice." She rummaged in her book bag and showed Nancy the small bottle of lotion.

Nancy nodded. "Is that why you dropped your apple? Because you're the one who is making a mess of the pumpkin contest?"

CHAPTER NINE

Starry Shenanigans

"Wh-what?" Emma asked.

"It does make sense," George said. "You were so upset that you had to move to River Heights."

"And you don't seem to like your aunt very much," Bess added.

Emma shook her head. "No, no. I would never do anything like that." She paused. "I won't lie, I did think about doing something—not like what happened, but maybe hide her car keys so she couldn't go to some of those dumb meetings all the time." Emma closed her eyes as tears started to roll down her cheeks. "I just wished she was able to pay more attention to me and Audrey."

Nancy handed Emma a napkin. "I'm sorry,

I didn't mean to make you cry," Nancy said. "We're just trying to figure out who did all this before Saturday. You know that Mayor Strong will cancel the contest if we can't find out who stole the designs and ruined the festival!"

Emma wiped her eyes. "I guess I'm not surprised that you would think I did it," Emma said. "We should at least try to tell my aunt that you found the box of designs."

Later that day, Emma, George, Bess, and Nancy headed toward Miss Costello's house. Nancy was surprised to find out that it was only three blocks away from hers—they were practically neighbors!

They promised Hannah they would be home before dark. They were only allowed to walk five blocks from Nancy's house on their own, in daylight.

Nancy had brought a little bag with her that held both the headband and charm bracelet she had found. She hoped Aunt Claire would be more willing to talk to them this time.

When they finally arrived at the Costello house, it was a pretty bungalow, with a few flower beds in front. Of course, the flowers weren't out anymore, but Nancy imagined that they were probably very pretty once spring rolled around.

Emma unlocked the front door and had them come inside. It was very cozy, with pictures of Emma, Audrey, and people who Nancy assumed were Emma and Audrey's parents and other relatives all over the walls. Emma set out some milk and what looked like fresh chocolate chip cookies.

"My aunt is running a little late," Emma said. "She should be here in, like, ten minutes."

Out of the corner of her eye, Nancy noticed Audrey come down the staircase.

"Oh hey, guys," Audrey said. "Wanna come see my room?"

Emma scowled. "Audrey, not right now. We have important business to discuss!"

"Oh, it's okay," Bess said. "We have a little time before your aunt gets home."

Audrey gave her sister a smirk and led the four girls upstairs.

Audrey's room was definitely fit for a princess. There was pink wallpaper with sparkly purple butterflies. A bookshelf was in the corner, crammed with dozens of books, and there was a small, white, four-poster bed with an actual canopy over it.

As Audrey chatted away, showing the girls her space, Nancy noticed a doll on Audrey's bed. With a start, she realized the doll was wearing the same star charm bracelet as the one Nancy had in her bag.

Nancy casually walked over to the bed and picked up the doll.

Audrey was in the middle of showing George and Bess her cool mini-car (pink, of course) when she noticed Nancy looking at the doll.

"Oh, that's Anna," she said. "She's my Just Like Me doll."

"Oh really?" Nancy asked, trying to secretly take the bracelet off the doll. "That's pretty cool."

"Yeah!" Audrey said excitedly. "You can get her to have the same hair and eye color as you, and you can pick out all sorts of fun clothes and stuff for her. You can even get matching outfits!"

Nancy stared at Audrey as she pulled the star charm bracelet from her bag. "And it looks like you can even get matching jewelry, too," Nancy said.

George's and Bess's mouths dropped open. Emma looked confused.

"Wait, Audrey, isn't that the bracelet you've been missing?" Emma asked.

Audrey's eyes grew wide. "Wow! Yeah! That's my charm bracelet." She took a few tentative steps toward Nancy. "Wh-where did you find it?"

"I found it in the tent right after everything was destroyed," Nancy replied. "So *you* were the one who wrecked everything!"

Audrey looked down at her feet and didn't say anything.

"Audrey? Is that true?"

All the girls looked up to see Aunt Claire in the doorway to Audrey's room, looking sad.

Audrey finally looked up at everyone. "I didn't mean to ruin everything, I swear! I just got so mad that I couldn't decorate and have fun like everyone else because of that stupid rule. So I figured I'd make one just for myself.

"During the opening ceremony, there wasn't really anyone around in the actual tent, since we'd set up most of the stuff the day before," Audrey continued. "I snuck back in and tried to get some paint to use and accidentally tipped the box of bottles over. The paint spilled all over one of the tables and knocked down a bunch of pumpkins, making such a mess! I got scared that Aunt Claire would come in and get mad at me for ruining things."

She glanced at her aunt. "When I went to run out, some other stuff got messed up too, but I didn't mean it, I promise!"

Everyone looked around, puzzled. "But what about the missing design forms?" Aunt Claire asked quizzically. "Did you do all of that too?"

Nancy looked up at Aunt Claire sheepishly. "Well, we actually came here to tell you that we found the box of forms by the bank on Main Street," she confessed. "But a few of them got ripped up."

Aunt Claire looked surprised. "You found them? How?"

The Clue Crew exchanged smiles. "We followed the paper trail," Nancy explained. "Really—the wind blew a piece of one of the forms toward us, and we just kept picking up pieces until we found the box with the rest of the entries."

Aunt Claire rubbed her eyes.

"Well, we can't use those, but at least we kind

of know what happened. And, missy, you are still in big trouble," Aunt Claire said, looking at Audrey with a stern expression. "You should have been honest with me at the start. But it looks like there is still one more person—or people—that we need to find!"

"Audrey, did you see anyone else go in after you left?" Emma asked.

Audrey shook her head. "I didn't see anyone, but I was trying to get out quickly through the back of the tent," she explained. She looked at Aunt Claire. "Does this mean I can't go to the festival again this weekend? Or get another accessory for Anna, like you said I could?"

"Yes to the festival, no to the doll stuff," Aunt Claire said with a smile. "I think she's gotten you into enough trouble so far!"

Everyone laughed as they headed back downstairs. But Nancy was still worried. With only a few more days left until the last weekend of the festival, there was still a pumpkin problem they needed to solve!

Chapter Ten

Dance Doozy

On Saturday morning, Nancy woke up to whistling.

"Time to wake up, Nancy!" Mr. Drew said cheerfully. "I've got waffles cooking!"

Nancy groaned and rolled over. "Just a few more minutes, Daddy," she said sleepily.

"But I have to get you to the festival! Hopefully they have some more information and you can do the contest anyway," Mr. Drew said.

With that, Nancy was wide awake. The last weekend of the festival! She followed her dad downstairs to the kitchen table, where he had put out another impressive breakfast spread, just like the weekend before.

"How's the case going, Nancy?" Mr. Drew asked. "Have you found any more clues that might help Miss Costello figure out who stole the designs?" Though Nancy had let him know that they discovered who destroyed all the supplies, they still weren't sure who stole the entry forms.

"Well, we really don't know," Nancy said. "The only other clue we have is that headband from the new shop. But that really doesn't help us."

"What about that Deirdre girl you were talking about earlier?" Mr. Drew asked. "Didn't you think she had something to do with it?"

"I did, especially since her initials were in the band. But it wasn't her," Nancy said. "She said it had a different shimmer than the band she had lost."

Mr. Drew chuckled. "Oh, you girls are funny with your accessories. When you were little, all you wanted were bows in your hair, all the time. Always two! Your mom would get upset if I didn't match them up, but you always insisted on having two bows."

Nancy smiled. She loved hearing stories about her as a baby—and loved hearing stories with her mom even more.

After cleaning up breakfast, Mr. Drew went to pick up George and Bess, and all four of them headed downtown. It was another beautiful fall day—sunny and on the warmer side.

"The committee definitely lucked out with the weather for the past week," Mr. Drew commented. "It's been perfect for outside activities!"

Nancy sighed. "Yeah, and it is perfect for pumpkin decorating too. If we could have a contest!"

Mr. Drew patted Nancy's shoulder. "Don't worry, Nancy. I'm sure they'll have something figured out before the festival is over. I can't imagine them canceling the whole thing!"

The fair was already bustling when they got there. All the vendors were open and the food stalls were doing brisk business, selling all sorts of treats to hungry fairgoers.

"It looks like there's going to be a show

soon," George said, pointing at the main stage. "People are starting to line up."

Nancy nodded. "There's supposed to be a show every hour today," she said. "Lots of dance schools and stuff like that."

Mr. Drew pointed toward the fried dough booth that was right near the stage. "Why don't we get a little treat and go watch the first show?" he suggested.

As the group made their way to buy their snack, Nancy noticed that the first act looked like a dance studio. Nancy recognized some of the girls from school, who were a year behind her. They were wearing shiny gold costumes, with tap shoes and long, matching gold gloves.

As Nancy looked a little closer, she also noticed something else. All the girls were wearing shiny, gold headbands—just like the one that Nancy had found on the ground near the missing entry forms!

All the girls—except for one.

Nancy nudged her dad.

"Daddy? I think I know who might have stolen the designs."

George, Bess, Nancy, and Mr. Drew rushed up to the group of dancers.

"Can I help you?" A woman about Aunt Claire's age walked over. "I'm Anne, the dance teacher for this group."

Nancy held out the headband she had brought with her, just in case. "I think your dancer is missing this headband."

Anne looked at the headband in surprise. "Dana! Is this yours?"

Dana smiled. "Wow, where did you find that? I was wondering what happened to it!"

At that moment, Aunt Claire and Rick Rickston came over, with Emma and Audrey in tow.

"Hi. Is everything okay over here?" Aunt Claire asked, concerned.

Nancy held out the headband. "This was found right next to the box of stolen design forms," Nancy said.

Dana looked shocked. "I didn't take those! I never would have taken them!" she said.

"That's because I did," someone said behind them. Tommy Sassano!

"Tommy? What on earth is going on here?" asked Mr. Rickston.

Nancy looked at Mr. Rickston in surprise. "You know Tommy?" Nancy asked.

Mr. Rickston nodded. "Tommy and Dana are my nephew and niece," he explained.

"So that means Tommy

and Dana couldn't enter, just like Emma and Audrey," Nancy said, thinking aloud.

Tommy nodded. "When I found out that we couldn't enter, I got so mad. Everyone else was talking about the designs. So during the opening part of the ceremony, I snuck in with Dana's dance bag and grabbed the forms. Her headband must have fallen out when I took them out."

Nancy shook her head. "But, Tommy, that's not fair to everyone else," she said.

Tommy shrugged. "I know. After I took them, I knew that I shouldn't have done it. And I know how hard my uncle and your aunt Claire worked on the festival," he said, looking at Audrey and Emma. "But I was just so jealous that every other kid in River Heights got to do this and I didn't!"

"But why didn't you just put the forms back the next day?" Bess pointed out.

"I was going to, I swear," Tommy said. "But then it was hard to get down to the festival during the week, since my mom and dad don't like me going here by myself, and they couldn't drop me off. And by the time I went to get the forms, a bunch had blown away or gotten ripped. I was scared about getting in trouble," he explained. He looked at his uncle. "I'm really sorry, Uncle Rick."

Mr. Rickston sighed and gave his nephew a half smile. "Well, we will definitely have to talk to Mom and Dad about this. But I am sorry that you felt so upset about not being able to enter."

Aunt Claire nodded. "It must have been hard to see all your friends working on this," she agreed. "How about you guys decorate a pumpkin, just for fun, tomorrow? We can still put them out, but they can't be considered for the winning entry."

At that, everyone perked up. "You mean that the competition is back on?" Nancy asked eagerly.

Aunt Claire smiled. "Well, I need to double-check with Mayor Strong, but I'm sure we can do it before the end of the festival. I'll have him make an announcement. We just need to get all the replacement supplies to the tent!"

The Clue Crew, along with several other kids, cheered.

"I'm glad we can still have the contest, Miss Costello," Nancy said. "Think we can help you with getting everything together?"

Aunt Claire grinned. "I'll have the fritters waiting!"

A few nights later, Nancy snuggled in bed with her trusty notebook and Chip. Her pumpkin, which had a very sparkly Chip face painted on it, sat on her desk. With a contented sigh, Nancy began to write:

Well, the Clue Crew has solved another case: the pumpkin puzzle!

Emma, Audrey, Dana, and Tommy ended up having a lot of fun, even though they weren't able to be in the competition. Audrey and

Tommy are grounded forever, but Aunt Claire and Uncle Rick didn't seem too upset in the end.

We helped round up all the contestants and supplies, and the contest happened the last day of the festival. Madison ended up winning, but George came in second with her MusicMate design! And she will be featured on one of the flyers for next year's festival too!

Next year's festival will be even better! I can already taste the fritters. Mystery solved!

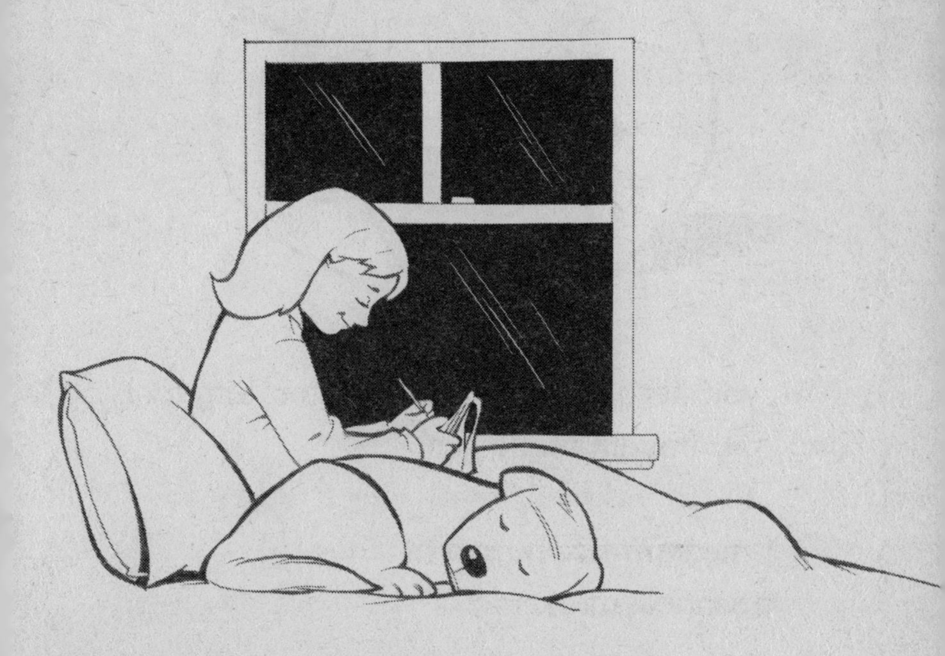

Pumpkin DIY

Nancy, Bess, and George had lots of fun coming up with cool pumpkin designs for the Fall Festival, and now you can too!

All you need are a few basic decorating tools and your imagination:

1 medium-size pumpkin
Washable markers

Permanent felt-tip markers

Scissors

Stencils with different designs

Ribbon and decorative cloth, various sizes and patterns

Glitter pens

Beads and buttons of various sizes

Nontoxic spray paint

Glue gun

First, have an adult carve out the top of your pumpkin. Scoop out the seeds and "innards" of the pumpkin.

Next, sketch out your design on the pumpkin using the washable markers. They are perfect because if you make a mistake or want to start over, it's easy to erase!

Once you have the design sketched out, it's time to go crazy! You can draw in a basic jack-o'-lantern design, or make it more personal. Bedazzle your pumpkin with your initials, make a pretty pattern with the ribbon, or make the shape of your favorite animal.

Some ideas and tips:

- You can fill in the design with more of the washable markers, if you want it to be a solid color.
- Spray paint adds a fun, shiny effect to your pumpkin. Make sure you are in a well-ventilated area when you use it! Have an adult nearby to help.
- Add fun, sparkly touches with the different ribbon and glitter pens. Make sure the ribbon/decorative cloth stays put by using the glue gun, and make sure a grown-up helps you warm up the glue beforehand.

Tasty Hint: After the pumpkin seeds are scooped out of the pumpkin, ask a grown-up to help you roast them for a tasty fall snack!

Preheat the oven to 300 degrees F. Toss the seeds with two to three teaspoons of melted butter and a seasoning of your choice. You can season them with salt and pepper, cinnamon and sugar, garlic, or any other spice, or just have them plain. Spread them out evenly in a shallow cookie sheet or baking pan and roast for about forty-five minutes or until golden brown, stirring occasionally. Yummy!

Nancy Drew and the Clue Crew

Test your detective skills with more Clue Crew cases!

#1 *Sleepover Sleuths*
#2 *Scream for Ice Cream*
#3 *Pony Problems*
#4 *The Cinderella Ballet Mystery*
#5 *Case of the Sneaky Snowman*
#6 *The Fashion Disaster*
#7 *The Circus Scare*
#8 *Lights, Camera . . . Cats!*
#9 *The Halloween Hoax*
#10 *Ticket Trouble*
#11 *Ski School Sneak*
#12 *Valentine's Day Secret*
#13 *Chick-napped!*
#14 *The Zoo Crew*
#15 *Mall Madness*
#16 *Thanksgiving Thief*
#17 *Wedding Day Disaster*
#18 *Earth Day Escapade*
#19 *April Fool's Day*
#20 *Treasure Trouble*
#21 *Double Take*
#22 *Unicorn Uproar*
#23 *Babysitting Bandit*
#24 *Princess Mix-up Mystery*
#25 *Buggy Breakout*
#26 *Camp Creepy*
#27 *Cat Burglar Caper*
#28 *Time Thief*
#29 *Designed for Disaster*
#30 *Dance Off*
#31 *The Make-a-Pet Mystery*
#32 *Cape Mermaid Mystery*
#33 *The Pumpkin Patch Puzzle*

FROM ALADDIN • PUBLISHED BY SIMON & SCHUSTER

Life in the White House will never be the same!

Candy Fairies

Visit
candyfairies.com
for more delicious
fun with your
favorite fairies.

Play games, download activities, and so much more!

EBOOK EDITIONS ALSO AVAILABLE

FROM ALADDIN • KIDS.SIMONANDSCHUSTER.COM